CINDER-ELLY

by **Frances Minters**

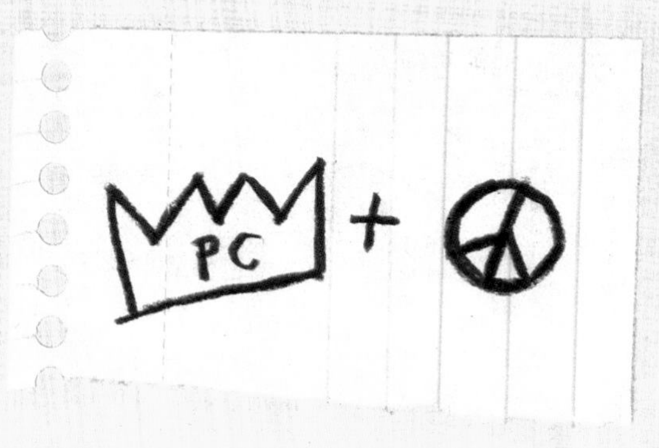

illustrated by **G. Brian Karas**

PUFFIN BOO

To my mother, Betty Gamer Caplan,
and to Arthur

—F.M.

To Paige, with thanks

—G.B.K.

PUFFIN BOOKS
Published by the Penguin Group
Penguin Books USA Inc., 345 Hudson Street, New York, New York 10014, U.S.A.
Penguin Books Ltd, 27 Wrights Lane, London W8 5TZ, England
Penguin Books Australia Ltd, Ringwood, Victoria, Australia
Penguin Books Canada Ltd, 10 Alcorn Avenue, Toronto, Ontario, Canada M4V 3B2
Penguin Books (N.Z.) Ltd, 182-190 Wairau Road, Auckland 10, New Zealand

Penguin Books Ltd, Registered Offices:
Harmondsworth, Middlesex, England

First published in the United States of America by
Viking, a division of Penguin Books USA Inc., 1994
Published in Puffin Books, 1997

20 19 18 17 16 15

THE LIBRARY OF CONGRESS HAS CATALOGED THE VIKING EDITION AS FOLLOWS:

Minters, Frances.
Cinder-Elly / by Frances Minters ; illustrated by G. Brian Karas.
p. cm.
Summary: In this rap version of the traditional fairy tale,
the overworked younger sister gets to go to a basketball game and meets
a star player, Prince Charming.
ISBN 0-670-84417-9
[1. Fairy tales. 2. Folklore. 3. Stories in rhyme.] I. Karas, G. Brian, ill.
II. Title.
PZ8.3.M655Ci 1994 398.21—dc20 [E] 93-14533 CIP AC

Puffin Books ISBN 0-14-056126-9

Manufactured in China

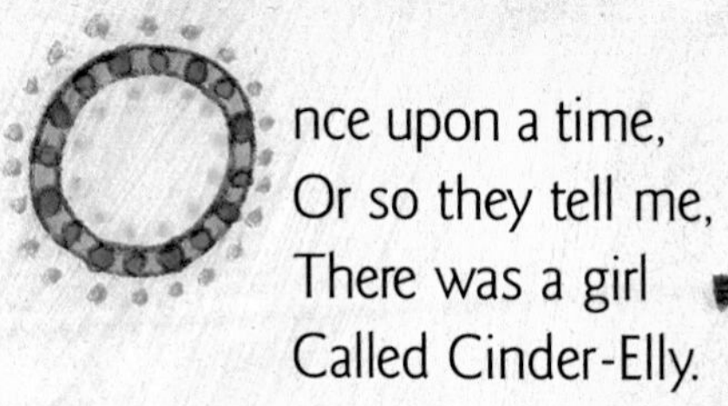

Once upon a time,
Or so they tell me,
There was a girl
Called Cinder-Elly.

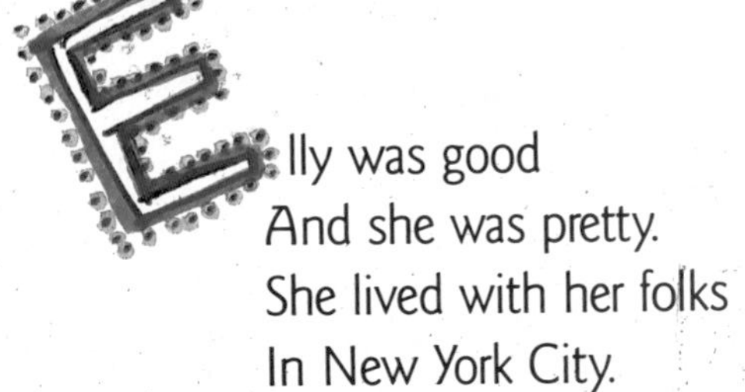

Elly was good
And she was pretty.
She lived with her folks
In New York City.

With Mom and Dad
And Sue and Nelly.
Her sisters were mean
To Cinder-Elly.

When school let out
They'd watch TV.
They'd ask Cinder-Elly
To serve iced tea.

Or else they'd play
A video game.
But they never asked Elly
To do the same.

Sometimes when Elly
Was washing the floor
They'd slide across it
And out the door.

What do you think
Would happen then?
Why, Elly would have
To wash it again!

SHOCKING!

Elly cleaned up
'Cause she liked to be neat
From the hair on her head
To the toes on her feet.

She worked so hard,
It was a pity
She had no fun
In New York City.

DON'T FRET, ELLY. THINGS
WILL GET BETTER SOON.

But then one day
El got a note.
So did her sisters.
Somebody wrote:

"Sue, El, and Nelly,
We picked your name.
You've won free tickets
To a basketball game."

I TOLD YOU THINGS WOULD
GET BETTER.

to: SUE, NELLY, and ELLY

"We accept with pleasure,"
Said Sue and Nelly.
"And I do, too,"
Said Cinder-Elly.

Her sisters just looked
At her and smiled.
And then they said,
"You can't go, child."

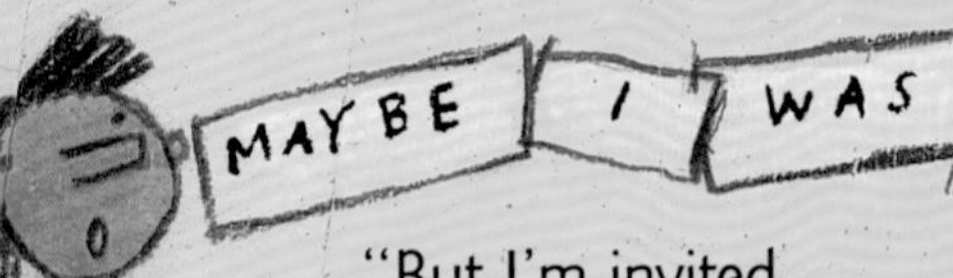

"But I'm invited,
It says so there."
"You're too young, Elly,
And you've nothing to wear."

"I'll shop," said Elly.
"But you've no money."
Elly's mother agreed,
"They're so right, honey.

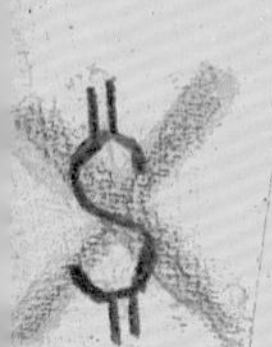

"There's no money for three
Only money for two.
Let your sisters go, Elly,
They're older than you."

So Elly's big sisters
Went right out shopping
And Elly stayed home
And did the mopping.

POOR CINDER-ELLY

The night of the game
As El watched them go,
An old lady came by
And said, "Elly, hello."

"Excuse me," said El,
"But I know all the dangers.
I'm never allowed
To speak to strangers."

"I'm your godmother, Elly.
Don't you recognize me?
Last time I saw you
You were two or three."

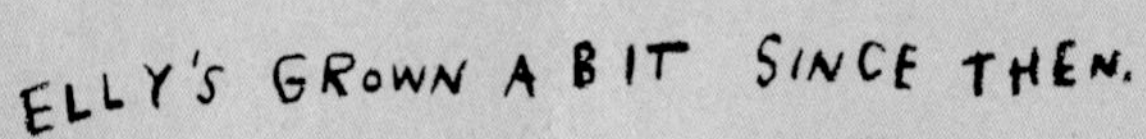

ELLY'S GROWN A BIT SINCE THEN.

"I'm here because
We have things to do.
Keep your eyes on my cane
I have something for you."

WHAT COULD IT BE?

She waved her cane once;
El squealed like a flute.
Her clothes had turned into
A basketball suit!

"And here's something else
To go with your clothes—
Glass sneakers," said Godma
"You'll need two of those."

"Now wait, Godmother!
Hold on a minute.
I'm just *watching* the game.
I don't want to be in it."

"Oops!" said the lady.
"Excuse my mistake.
Let's see what else
My cane can make."

And *poof!* Elly wore
A satiny shirt
With a beautiful, flowery,
Red miniskirt.

YOU LOOK GREAT, EL!

Elly was happy
'Cause she looked so fine.
"Now go to the game,
And have a good time."

"Thank you, dear Godma,
I'm glad that you came.
But how am I going
To get to the game?"

"That's an easy one, dear,
I've got a plan.
I'll send you off
On this old garbage can."

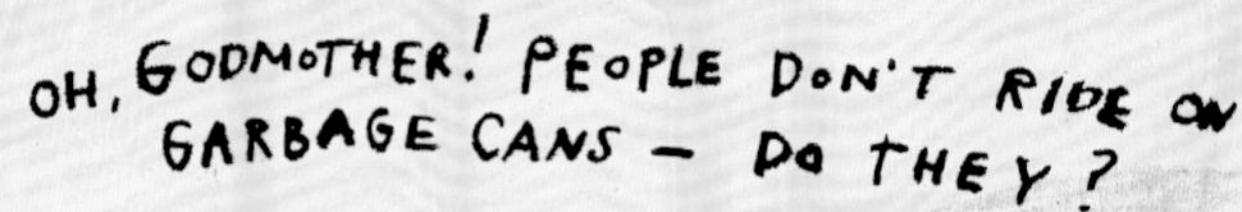

OH, GODMOTHER! PEOPLE DON'T RIDE ON GARBAGE CANS — DO THEY?

She waved her cane
And said, "Kerplike!"
The garbage can
Became a bike!

El got right on
And almost fell off,
'Cause riding a bike
In glass sneakers is tough.

"You'll be fine, El,
I know that is true.
There's just one thing
I ask of you.

"Be home by ten,
Or else, my dear,
Your pretty new clothes
Will disappear."

OH, OH!

“No problem,” purred Elly,
As sweet as a kitty.
Then she rode off
Through New York City.

The game was just starting
When El got to her seat.
Out ran Prince Charming.
People rose to their feet.

SO THAT'S THE FAMOUS PRINCE CHARMING!

“Let's go, Prince Charming!”
El yelled with the rest.
Of all her school's players,
Prince was the best.

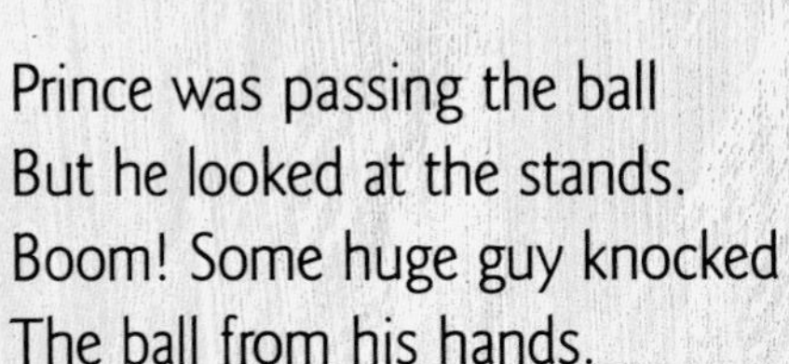

Prince was passing the ball
But he looked at the stands.
Boom! Some huge guy knocked
The ball from his hands.

Elly stood on her toes
And raised her arms fast.
She caught that ball
Before it flew past.

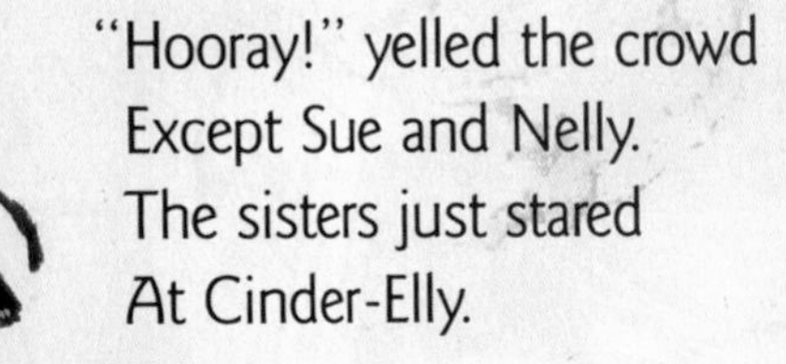

"Hooray!" yelled the crowd
Except Sue and Nelly.
The sisters just stared
At Cinder-Elly.

"Is that Elly?" asked Sue.
"No, that's a bad guess.
She's older than Elly
And much better dressed."

"Here's the ball!" Elly shouted,
As she threw it up high.
"In the future, be careful."
"Thanks, miss, I'll try."

Prince stared at Elly
And said, "Glad to meetcha.
After the game, let's
Go get some pizza."

"What's your name?" he asked.
"I can't tell you, I fear."
For El was afraid that
Her sisters might hear.

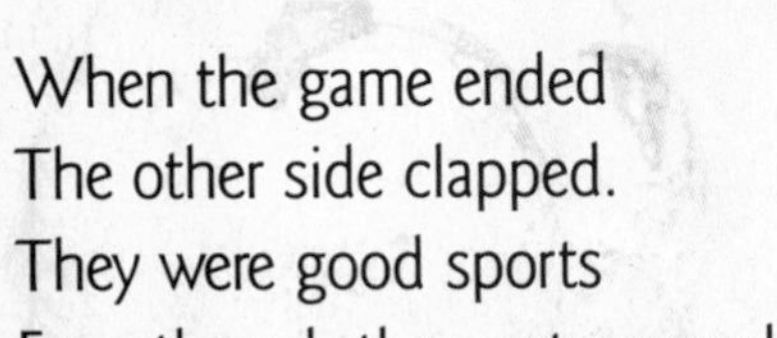

When the game ended
The other side clapped.
They were good sports
Even though they got zapped.

"Will you wait for me, please?"
Prince stopped by El's chair.
"I'll shower and change
And blow-dry my hair."

PRINCE

El stayed till the clock
Blinked **9:58**.
In two more minutes
She would be late.

She got up and ran.
It's sad, but it's true,
A lace came undone
And she lost a glass shoe.

But she couldn't stop now
So she hurried on.
All she saw was a trash can—
Her bike was gone.

I WAS AFRAID THIS WOULD HAPPEN.

Elly waved at the can
And she said, "Kerplike!"
But the can wouldn't change
Back into a bike.

Then she looked at her clothes.
"Oh, no! They're the same
As the ones I was wearing
'Fore Godmother came."

She waved at her clothes.
Poof! They didn't change either.
"Where's Godma?" she wondered,
"Now that I need her?"

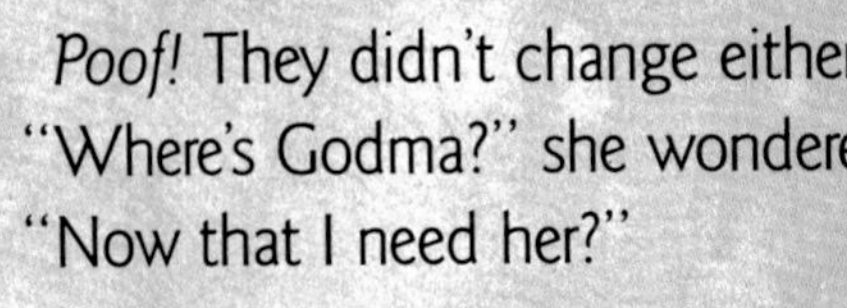

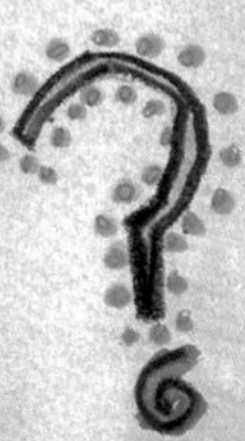

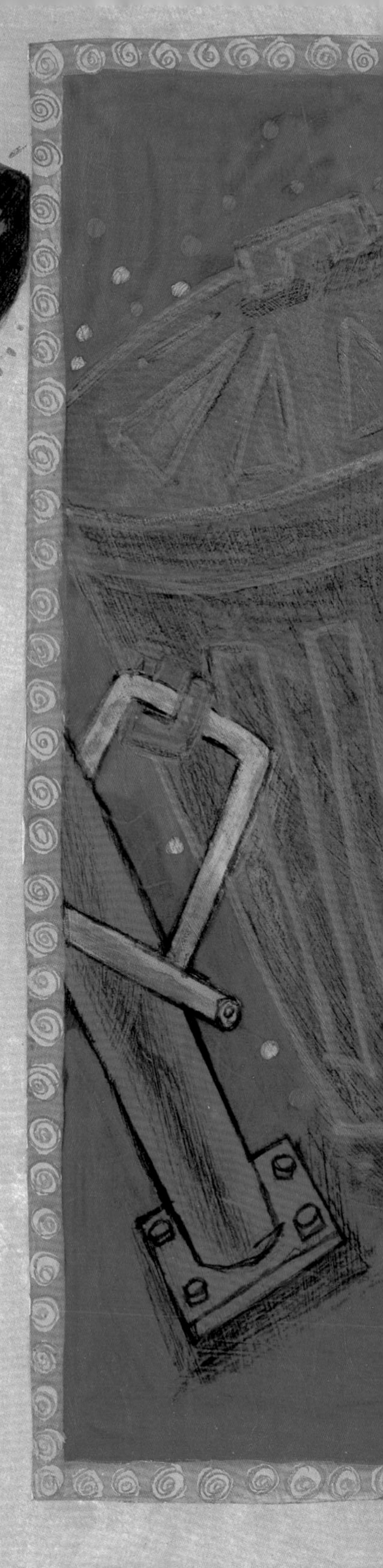

Meanwhile, Prince Charming,
Looking pretty cool,
Was busy signing photos
For the fans at school.

When he was finished,
He looked all about.
Elly wasn't inside
So Prince went out.

Outside he saw no one
Just some girl who ran
Off down the street with
A huge garbage can.

But on the steps he spied
One sparkly shoe.
"This sneaker," said Charming,
"Gives me a clue."

WHY DOES PRINCE CHARMING
NEED THE SHOE?

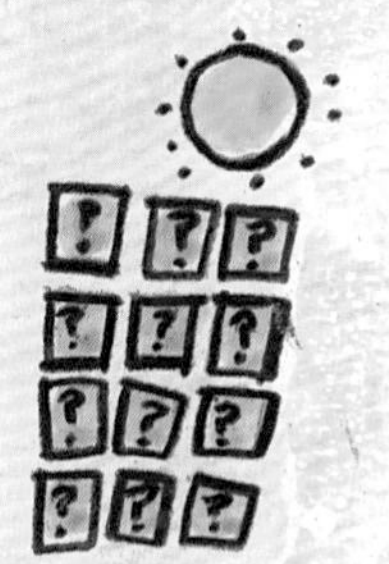

Next morning Cinder-Elly
Tried giving Prince a call
But his number wasn't listed
In the book at all.

At the same time, Charming
Sat at a table.
He drew the sneaker
As well as he was able.

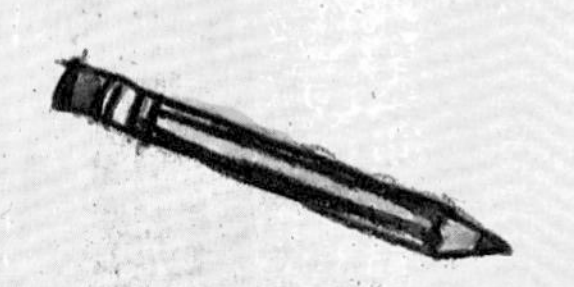

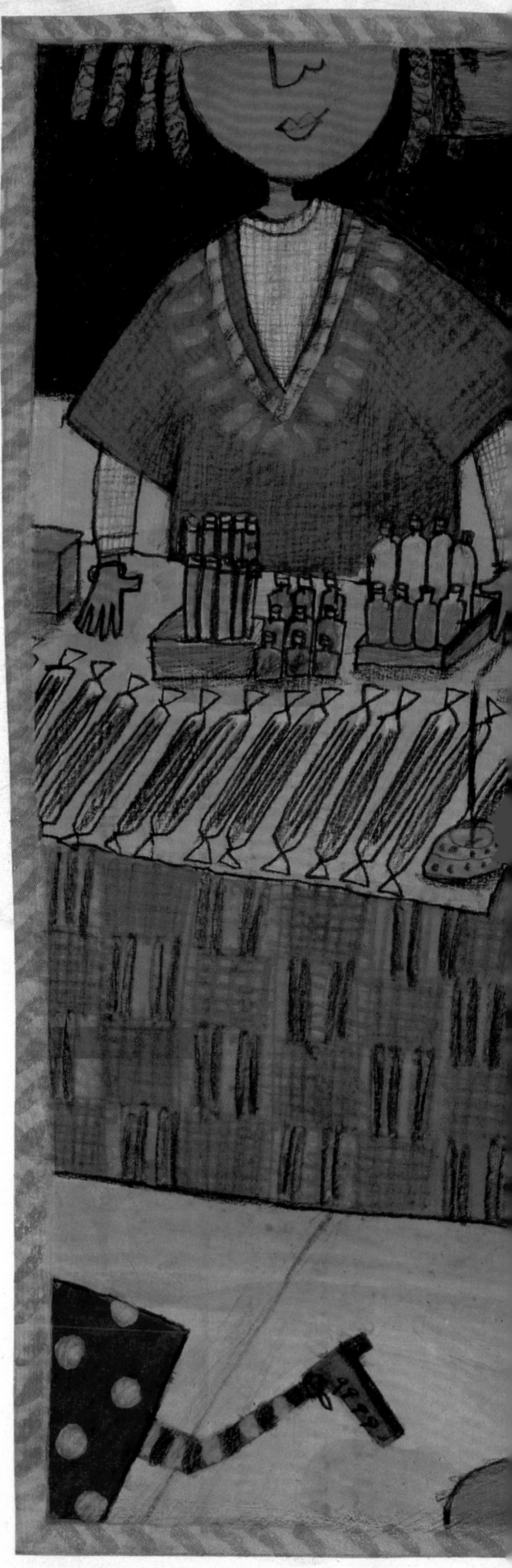

Beneath it he wrote
For all to see,
"If you lost this sneaker,
Please telephone me."

Then he wrote his name
And phone number, too.
He went to the copy shop
To print a few.

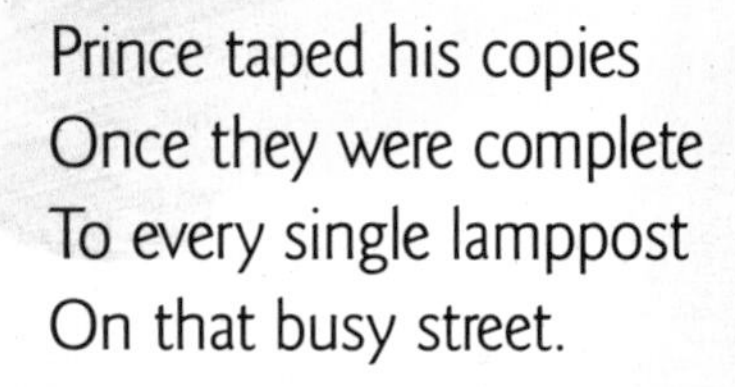

Prince taped his copies
Once they were complete
To every single lamppost
On that busy street.

Many women phoned him,
With feet too big or small.
Prince Charming wasn't happy.
"Won't the right one ever call?"

Hey, gang! Look out!
Here's Sue, here's Nelly
With the poster to show
To Cinder-Elly.

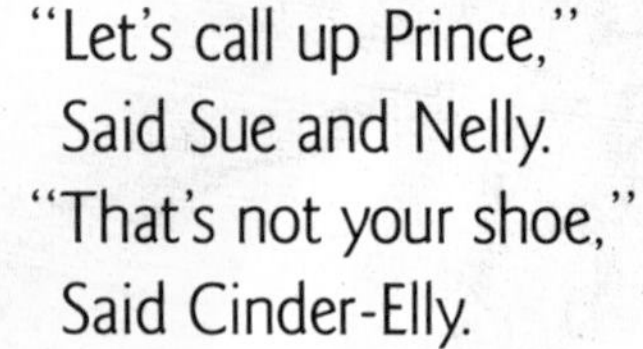

"Let's call up Prince,"
Said Sue and Nelly.
"That's not your shoe,"
Said Cinder-Elly.

IF YOU LOST
THIS SNEAKER
PLEASE
TELEPHONE ME.
PRINCE CHARMING
555-0009
IF YOU LOST
THIS SNEAKER
PLEASE
TELEPHONE ME

"Oh, no?" they said.
"But we'll try it, since
How else could we ever
Meet a real, live prince?"

They phoned Prince Charming
And just as they planned
He dropped in to visit
With the sneaker in hand.

Prince was surprised
By Nelly and Sue.
He said, "I don't remember
Either of you."

Sue tried the shoe
And fell down flat.
"Poor Sue," laughed Nell,
"Your foot's too fat."

Next Nelly tried
And went into a tizzy.
The shoe was so tight
It made her feel dizzy.

SERVES THEM BOTH RIGHT!

Then Elly came out
From where she'd been looking.
Her sisters yelled, "Elly,
Go back to your cooking."

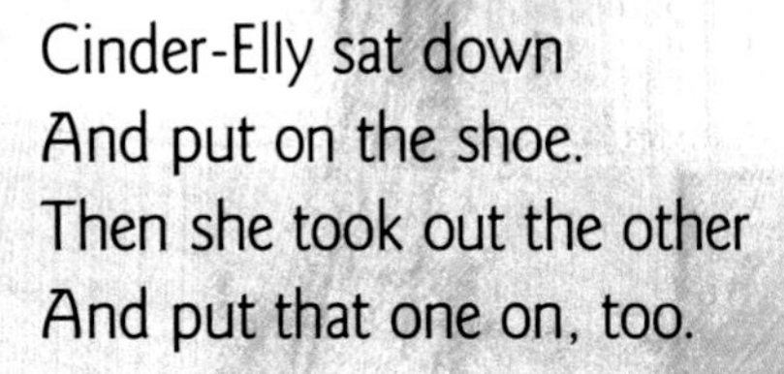

Cinder-Elly sat down
And put on the shoe.
Then she took out the other
And put that one on, too.

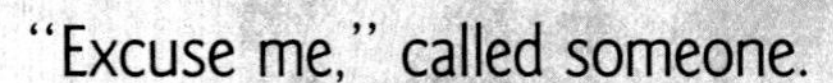

"Excuse me," called someone.
"May I come in?"
"Please do," said Elly.
"Godma, where have you been?"

"I've been busy," she answered,
"But I know my duty
To see Cinder-Elly
And her friend Prince Cutie."

"Prince Charming," he corrected.
"Well, how do you do?
It's time you saw Elly
In the clothes that you knew."

Poof! Poof! she waved.
Elly's clothes became
The ones she had worn
To the basketball game.

"Yikes!" screamed the sisters.
"Shush!" Godmother told them.
"You deserve a good scolding."
And she started to scold them.

PC

"You're forgiven," said Elly,
"I'm sure that you've seen
That it's awfully wrong
To be terribly mean."

"You're right, Cinder-Elly.
And we promise we know it.
If ever we feel mean again,
We just won't show it."

Prince said to Elly,
"Let's go spread the news."
"Wait, Prince," said Elly,
"Till I change my shoes."

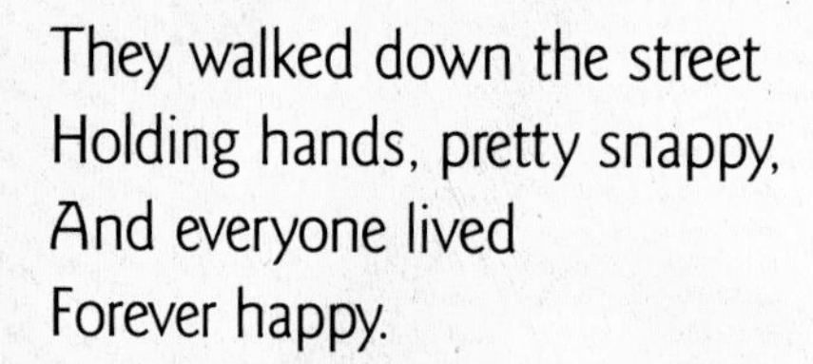

They walked down the street
Holding hands, pretty snappy,
And everyone lived
Forever happy.

I'M SO GLAD EVERYTHING TURNED OUT
ALL RIGHT. AREN'T YOU?

PC

TAXI